Coral Reef Rescue

The Sea Keepers series

The Mermaid's Dolphin

The Sea Unicorn

Coral Reef Rescue

Sea Turtle School

Penguin Island

Coral Reef Rescue

CORAL RIPLEY

First U.S. edition published by Sourcebooks Young Readers in 2021.

Published by Sourcebooks Young Readers, an imprint of Sourcebooks Kids
P.O. Box 4410, Naperville, Illinois 60567-4410
(630) 961-3900
sourcebookskids.com

Originally published in 2020 in Great Britain by Orchard Books, an imprint of Hachette UK Children's Group, part of the Watts Publishing Group Limited.

The Library of Congress Cataloging-in-Publication data is on file with the publisher.

Source of Production: Sheridan Books, Chelsea, Michigan, United States
Date of Production: March 2021
Run Number: 5021161

Printed and bound in the United States of America.
SB 10 9 8 7 6 5 4 3 2 1

Special thanks to Sarah Hawkins.

For Annabelle Emery,

my lovely goddaughter.

Chapter One

Grace took a deep breath and looked down at the bright blue water. She was standing with her toes at the edge of the swimming pool, the familiar smell of chlorine in her nose, and her swimming cap tight over her long blond hair. At the side of the pool, her coach gave her a thumbs-up. Grace never normally felt nervous, but her team, the Dashing Dolphins, had been training for this competition for ages, and she really wanted to do well.

She shook her hands and legs, trying to loosen up.

"Go, Grace, go! Go, Grace, go!"

Grace grinned as she heard her best friends chanting. She looked up at the stands and finally spotted them. Layla was wearing a glittery top that caught the light as she jumped up and down, and Emily was twisting her curly hair around her finger. Next to them was Grace's mom, her hair in a messy bun and her glasses perched on the end of her nose, her granddad with his bushy white hair, and her little brother, Henry, who was in his swimming shorts and waving at her. "Just do your best!" Mom called, crossing her fingers. Grace nodded and pulled the goggles down over her eyes.

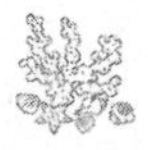

“Take your marks,” the announcer said. Grace raised her arms over her head and focused on the water. “Ready...go!”

As the horn sounded, Grace dove into the water and kicked as hard as she could. She knew she was a fast swimmer—but was she fast enough? She was aware of the girl in the next lane pulling ahead of her. If only

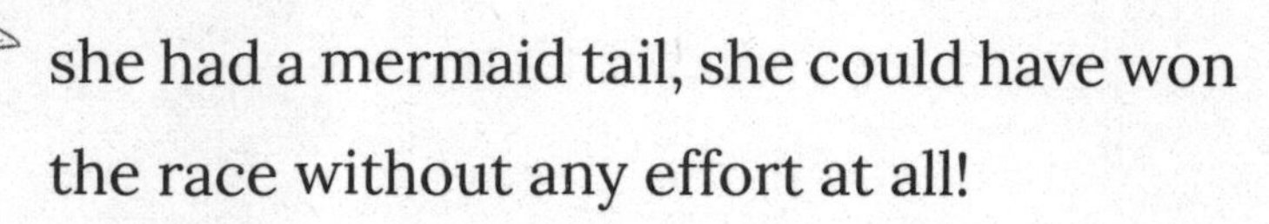

she had a mermaid tail, she could have won the race without any effort at all!

Grace tried to concentrate. She couldn't be a mermaid, but maybe she could *think* like one. Shutting her eyes, she imagined that she had to swim as fast as she could, because there was a shark chasing her! Grace kicked her legs and pulled her arms through the water, imagining sharp teeth gnashing right behind her. She kicked her feet harder and harder, swimming faster and faster—until suddenly she touched the side of the pool. Catching her breath, she heard a cheer from the stands. She'd won!

"That was incredible!" her coach said, hurrying up to her with a towel as she pulled herself out of the pool. "That was your personal best!"

"And the winner is Grace Ryback!" the announcer cried.

In the stands, Grace's friends and family were all cheering. Grace rushed over to them, dripping and grinning.

"You swam like a mermaid!" Mom said, wrapping her in a big hug.

"There's no such thing as mermaids," Henry scoffed.

"I wouldn't be so sure!" Granddad said, his eyes twinkling. "Did I ever tell you about the time my fishing boat was caught in a storm and I heard the most beautiful singing..."

Mom grinned and shook her head as Granddad started telling his tale, Henry staring up at him wide-eyed. As Granddad talked, Grace caught Layla and Emily's eyes,

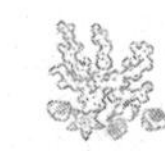

and they shared a secret smile. They knew that mermaids were real, because they had met them!

It had started when they'd rescued a dolphin from a fishing net. But Kai was no ordinary dolphin. He was the pet of a mermaid princess. Princess Marina had taken them to Atlantis, an underwater kingdom, hidden from human eyes by mermaid magic. Atlantis was in grave trouble, because an evil siren called Effluvia was threatening to take over the kingdom. To everyone's surprise, the three human girls had been chosen to become Sea Keepers—the only ones who could find the magical Golden Pearls and use their power to stop Effluvia.

"Go and get changed, Grace," Mom

interrupted her thoughts. "Henry's going to have his first lesson, and then we'll all go home for dinner."

"I thought you could already swim, Henry," Emily said.

Henry stood up and showed her his flippers, waddling along like a penguin. "I can! I'm learning to be a scuba diver!" he said excitedly, giving her a gap-toothed smile.

"He's not old enough to actually scuba dive," Grace's mom told them, "but he's going to start snorkeling. He's got his assessment with the teacher

today, and then he starts lessons next week."

"It's going to be great. I'm going to see lots of fish. Hey—I bet you don't know why the jellyfish blushed." Henry put a snorkel on. "Mmm-mam bur bua GAH!"

"What?" Layla said, laughing.

"Why *did* the jellyfish blush?" Emily asked curiously. "There's a jellyfish called a pink meanie, but I don't think it's pink because it's blushing..." She watched a lot of nature documentaries and knew lots of animal facts.

"Noooo!" Henry took the snorkel out of his mouth. "The jellyfish blushed because the sea WEED!" Laughing, he waddled over to where the sub-aqua club was setting up their scuba diving gear. Layla giggled.

"I can't believe I fell for that!" Emily groaned. Grace laughed as she took off her swimming cap and shook out her wet hair. As she did, she noticed something amazing—her shell bracelet was glowing!

Layla gasped, and Emily turned to them both with wide eyes. Their bracelets were shimmering too. That meant it was time for another mermaid adventure!

"Um, I need to get dressed," Grace said hurriedly.

"I'll come with you!" Layla said.

"Me too!" Emily agreed.

"Great, see you back here. Henry won't be long," Mom said.

"Okay!" Grace called as she, Emily, and Layla hurried away.

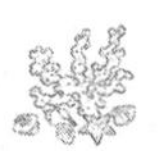

"The Mystic Clam must have remembered where another Golden Pearl is hidden!" Emily whispered as they rushed into the changing rooms and ducked inside a stall. No time would pass in the human world while they were away, but they didn't want anyone to see them magically disappear.

Grace grabbed her friends' hands as they looked down at their shining shell bracelets.

Together, they chanted:

"Take me to the ocean blue,
Sea Keepers to the rescue!"

Bubbles appeared in the air, swirling and surrounding them with magic. The air

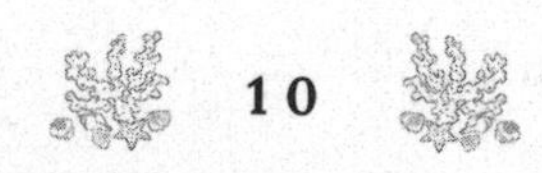

sparkled blue as the bubbles spun faster and faster. Then—*POP!*—they were underwater, the scales on their tails glittering in the crystal-clear sea. They were mermaids again!

Chapter Two

"Welcome back, Sea Keepers!" a mermaid said, swimming up to them. She had bright purple and pink hair, a lilac tail covered in tiny sparkling scales, and a crown made of shells.

"Marina!" Layla yelled, swishing her turquoise tail and swimming over to hug their mermaid friend.

Grace flicked her own tail and grinned as she zoomed through the water. Her tail was light pink with golden fins that matched her blond hair, and it was so fast! "Whoopee!" she shouted, swimming in a circle and back to her friends.

"I'm so pleased to see you!" Marina cried.

"What's wrong?" kindhearted Emily asked, flipping her yellow tail.

"Has Effluvia done something?" Grace asked. She couldn't bear the thought of the siren causing trouble.

"I'm okay, don't worry," Marina said, laughing. "My parents have gone on a royal tour of all the underwater kingdoms, and one of their royal dolphins was sick, so Kai went with them to pull the carriage."

"Oh, you must miss him," Emily said. The girls knew how much Marina loved her dolphin friend.

"That's not the worst thing—they left Prince Neptune in charge." Marina rolled her eyes. Grace grinned. Marina's older

brother was even more annoying than Henry!

"Ugh!" Layla said.

"I know!" Marina said. "He's been swimming around saying that he's the King of Atlantis and that I have to call him 'my lord.' If I don't, he doesn't answer! It's so nice to be away from him."

"Where *are* we?" Grace asked, looking around. "It's beautiful!"

They were by a coral reef, a huge bank covered in corals and sea anemones of every color. It was like an amazing under-water garden. Everywhere they looked, there were tropical fish darting busily in and out of the coral! She watched as a fish the size of a dinner plate swam past, and a family of orange and white clown fish

peeked out from behind a huge red anemone whose tentacles swayed in the clear turquoise water. Grace had lived next to the sea her whole life, but the fish at home didn't look anything like this!

"Hang on, is this the Great Barrier Reef?" Emily gasped in excitement. She reached out as if to touch one of the anemones, and its tentacles shrank back. "Oops, sorry! I didn't mean to scare you!"

Marina nodded.

"What's the Great Barrier Reef?" asked Grace, who preferred PE lessons to geography.

"It's off the coast of Australia," said Emily. "Lots of people go diving there. It's the biggest reef in the world—so big it can be seen from space."

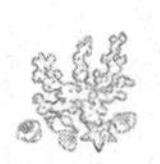

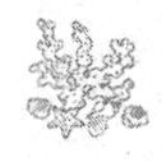

"Wow," Layla breathed, reaching out to stroke the coral. "That's amazing!"

"Not if you're looking for something tiny..." Grace said, touching the coral. It felt cool and light under her hand, like honeycomb. "Did the Mystic Clam remember that there's a Golden Pearl hidden here?" she asked Marina.

The Mystic Clam was one of the oldest creatures in the whole ocean. He had been there when the great battle between the mermaids and sirens was fought, and he was the only one who could remember where Marina's ancestor, Queen Nerissa, had hidden the Golden Pearls to protect them.

Marina nodded again, then recited:

"A great big brain will help you think.
Look for one of brightest pink."

"That riddle's too much for my tiny brain!" Layla joked. Grace nudged her friend with her tail. "You're smart and you know it!"

Layla had dyslexia and struggled with schoolwork sometimes, but she was clever in lots of ways—especially when it came to stopping Effluvia! Layla grinned and nudged Grace back. But as they laughed, they were interrupted by a strange wailing noise nearby.

Oohhnooooooooooooooooooooooooo! OoooOooooooOOOOOOo!

"What's that?" Layla asked.

"It sounds like someone crying," Emily gasped.

The girls looked around. There were fish everywhere, darting around the coral, but none of them looked upset. “I think it’s coming from the seabed,” Layla said, sounding confused.

Grace scoured the sandy floor, but she couldn’t see anything except rocks and shells. Then something twitched. An eye was poking out from the sand! “Hello? Is there someone there?” she asked.

The sand gave a little shake, and a ray appeared. It had a flat circular body with two googly eyes on top, wide fins that looked like wings, and a long flat tail. It was speckled exactly like the sand—no wonder they hadn't seen it!

"Are you okay?" Emily said gently.

The ray made the wailing noise again. "Ohhhhhhhhh! I wanted to be in the tropical talent show."

"Is that today?" Marina exclaimed. She turned to the girls. "The tropical talent show is one of the biggest events here at the reef. The Oceania mermaids put it on every year."

"That's not all." The ray fluttered his wings excitedly. "This year Queen Adrianna and King Caspian will be there, because it's the 200th show."

"I didn't know my parents were coming!" Marina said.

"You're Princess Marina?" the ray gasped. Sand flew everywhere as he buried himself again so only his googly eyes were showing. "Ooooohhhh, I'm not worthy!"

"Don't be silly," Marina said, laughing.

"Come out!" She coaxed the ray out of the sand. "I want to introduce you to the Sea Keepers—Grace, Emily, and Layla."

"I'm Raymond," the ray explained. He uncovered himself in a flurry of sand and swam in front of them, giving a funny dip that Grace guessed was supposed to be a bow. "It's an honor to meet you, Your Highness," he said, kissing her hand.

As he touched her, the ray's skin glowed blue and Marina jumped back. "Ouch!"

"Oh, I'm so sorry!" Raymond gasped. "I'm an electric ray. I can't believe I shocked the princess. Oh no, oh noooooo!" He burst into noisy tears and darted back down to the seabed.

"It's all right," Marina laughed before he could bury himself again. "I'm okay, I promise."

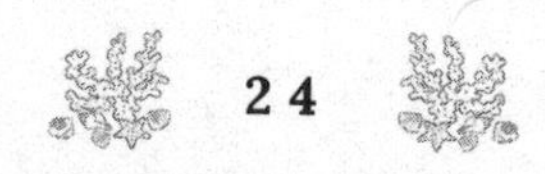

"Is that your talent?" Layla asked as the ray swam back up to them. Electricity rippled over Raymond's skin again.

He shook his head. "No, I'm a comedian. But I can't be in the show."

"Why not?" Grace asked.

"I've got stage fright," the ray admitted, his fins drooping sadly.

"Aw!" Layla went to stroke Raymond, but Grace stopped her just in time.

"Careful, you don't want to get shocked."

"Oops, I forgot!" Layla laughed. "I love jokes, Raymond, and I'm sure yours are great—why don't you practice on us?"

"And remember that the king and queen are just ordinary mermaids," Marina said. "They still have to brush their teeth

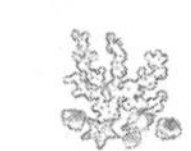

and polish their flippers, just like everyone else!"

But Raymond was looking up at her, starry-eyed. "I can't believe a real princess is talking to me!" he said.

"Well, this princess wants to hear some jokes!" Marina laughed. "Come on, show us your routine."

Raymond gave a cough and fixed his googly eyes on them. "Mermaids and mussels, turtles and tang, let me welcome you here today. What's a fish's favorite party game?"

"I don't know," Layla said, grinning. "What is it?"

"*Salmon* says!" Raymond grinned and shook his fins. The girls laughed politely.

"Why did the squid cross the reef?" Raymond asked.

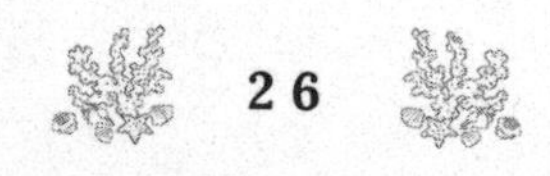

"Tell us," Marina encouraged him.

"To get to the other *tide!*" Raymond finished.

Grace leaned over to her friends. "His jokes are as bad as Henry's!" she whispered. The others giggled.

Each one of Raymond's jokes was worse than the last, but the little ray was so enthusiastic that it was funny anyway. "That's all for now!" Raymond finished, giving his funny bow. Marina and the girls applauded loudly.

"Wow, thank you," Raymond said. "Maybe I will enter the contest after all."

"My parents will love you," Marina promised him.

"I'd better go and tell the Oceania mermaids that I want to be in the show," Ray said.

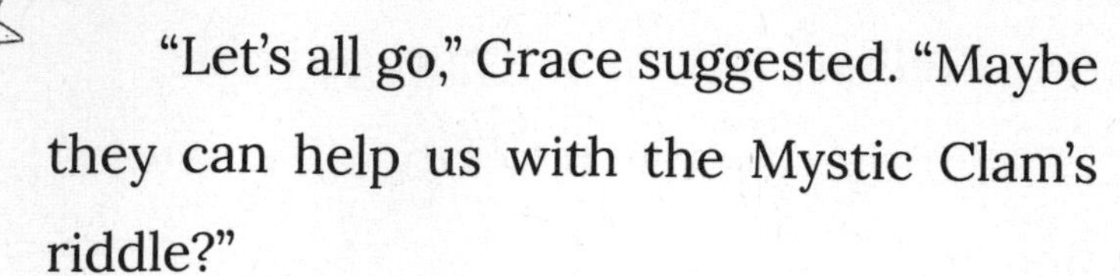

"Let's all go," Grace suggested. "Maybe they can help us with the Mystic Clam's riddle?"

"Yes!" Layla cheered. "Tropical talent show, here we come!"

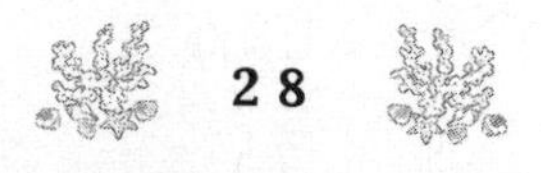

Chapter Three

Raymond led the way through the beautiful reef and into a clearing. Here, the coral had grown up into a huge arch, curving over a sandy stage marked out by shells. In front of the stage, there were hundreds of rocks laid out for seats. It was an incredible underwater theater!

As the girls stared in amazement, mermaids with brightly colored tails swam around, decorating the theater for the royal arrivals. On one side of the stage were two huge, throne-like rocks, covered with beautiful anemones in vibrant pinks and oranges. Mermaids were stringing seaweed garland across the coral arch, while, below, all kinds of sea creatures were practicing their acts.

"Look!" Emily cried. An octopus was juggling shells, all eight arms moving in different directions.

"I can't even juggle with two arms," Layla said with a laugh. "I would get so tangled up!"

On the other side of the stage, a pair of crabs were doing a complicated flamenco dance, clicking their pincers in time with the music drifting through the water from a crustacean band. The girls applauded

as the dance ended and the crabs took a bow. "These acts are really good!" Grace said.

Raymond gave a moan. "I can't compete with them!" he sobbed, and before the girls could stop him, he buried himself in the sand in front of the stage.

"Come on, Raymond, you can do it," Emily reassured him.

"No, I can't. Go away," came the ray's muffled voice.

As they were trying to convince Raymond to leave the sand, an Oceania mermaid with coral-pink hair and a turquoise tail came over, carrying a line of seaweed garland. "I'm sorry, we're not quite ready for the show yet. We're still preparing for it," she told them with a friendly smile.

"We're actually looking for a Golden Pearl," Grace explained. "We're the Sea Keepers, and this is Princess Marina." She introduced her friends, and the mermaid's smile grew even bigger.

"Welcome, Sea Keepers," she said. "I'm Tarni. And I'll help you however I can—we all will!"

Layla told Tarni about the riddle. "Has anyone seen a magical glow? Or do you know where we could find a pink brain?"

"A pink brain..." Tarni frowned and shook her head. "I can't think of anything like that. But there is someone who might know—my grandfather, Iluka. Shall I take you to him?"

"Oh, yes, please," Grace said.

Tarni started to lead the way, but first the girls swam to the seabed to talk to Raymond one more time. "Are you sure you won't come out?" Emily asked him.

"I'm sure, just go," he said.

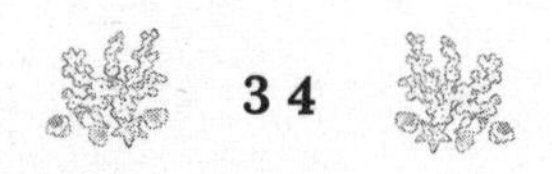

"We'll be back later," Grace promised, hoping the ray would change his mind.

Tarni led them through the great coral arch. Backstage, a group of mermaids and mermen were making seaweed garland. Sitting on a rock was an elderly merman with white hair, a long white beard, and a faded orange tail. "Grandpa, these are the Sea Keepers!" Tarni said as she swam forward to kiss his cheek.

"It's nice to meet you!" said Layla. "We love your beautiful reef. It's so colorful!"

"If you think it's colorful now, you should have seen it years ago," Iluka said, shaking his head.

"The seas are getting warmer, and the heat makes the coral sick and bleaches it white," Tarni explained.

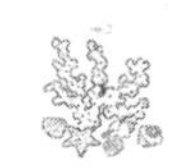

Emily, Layla, and Grace glanced at each other. Grace knew what her friends were thinking—it was because of climate change. They'd learned about it in school. Humans were making too many greenhouse gases, which were warming up the whole planet, causing problems on land and in the seas. They'd already seen it in the Arctic, where the ice was melting. It was obviously affecting the coral reef too!

"A sea turtle told me it's because of humans," Iluka said. "Is that right?"

Emily nodded sadly.

"But lots of people are trying to stop it," Layla added.

"Humans," Tarni said, sighing sadly. "They are always diving down to our reef and hurting the fragile coral."

Grace had a sudden thought. “How come they don’t see the theater?”

Iluka pointed a bony finger up to the surface. Looking closely, they could see a rainbow sheen—the theater was covered in a shimmering dome. Grace stared at it. It looked like—

"A bubble!" Layla burst out.

"It keeps the theater from human eyes and protects the coral too," Tarni explained. "Coral is hard, but it's very delicate. If people even gently touch it, they will hurt it."

"Oh no! We just touched the coral!" Emily gasped.

"It's okay when you're a mermaid," Marina reassured her. "Just don't ever touch it in your human form."

Tarni nodded. "Divers swim down to explore the reef. Sometimes they knock it accidentally with their artificial fins—" She glanced down at her tail. "What do you call those?"

"Flippers?" Grace suggested, thinking of her brother's diving gear.

"If they kick the coral with their flippers they can break it completely," Tarni said. "So we keep them away with the magical bubble. That way, our part of the reef is safe, and we can stay hidden from the humans."

That reminded Grace. They needed to find something else that was hidden—the Golden Pearl!

"Iluka, we need your help," she said, turning to the elderly merman.

Iluka sprang up from the rock. "What do you need? I can battle a swordfish or take on a manta ray with my fins tied behind my back!"

The girls giggled. "We need to solve a riddle from the Mystic Clam," Layla explained. "Maybe you can help us work out what it means?"

"Ah, the Mystic Clam!" Iluka said, chuckling. "That old scallop! He was thousands of years old when I was just a merboy. What is the riddle?"

"A *great big brain will help you think. Look for one of brightest pink*," Grace chanted hopefully.

"Hmmm..." Iluka scratched his head.

But just as they were all puzzling over the riddle, there was a commotion.

"Tarni, come quick!" a mermaid called. "Queen Adrianna and King Caspian are arriving!"

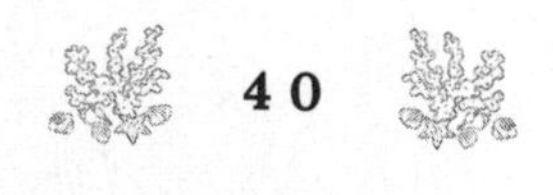

Chapter Four

Grace, Emily, Layla, and Marina hurried after the mermaids as they swam back through the coral arch and across the stage. The sea creatures had stopped rehearsing and were staring at the bubbles surging toward them through the turquoise water.

"The royal carriage must be coming!" one of the mermaids cried.

Grace watched excitedly, but, next to her, Emily twisted her tail nervously.

"Are you okay?" Grace whispered.

“Will they be upset that we haven’t found the pearl?” Emily asked.

Grace thought back to when they’d first met Marina’s parents. Queen Adrianna had been furious that Marina had brought humans into the mermaid world. She’d been even angrier when they’d been chosen to be the Sea Keepers. But they’d found two pearls since then...

“We haven’t found the pearl yet—but we *will*!” she said confidently.

Emily nodded.

All the mermaids bowed low as the flurry of bubbles cleared.

“Hang on, that’s not the royal carriage,” Marina muttered.

“What a magnificent welcome for little old me!” A beautiful voice rang through the

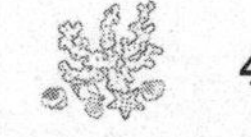

water like a bell. Grace felt a chill shiver down her tail. There was only one person who sounded so lovely but was actually horrible—Effluvia!

The siren swam out of the bubbles, followed by her pet anglerfish, Fang. As ugly as Effluvia was beautiful, Fang had huge crooked teeth and a light that hung over her face. Effluvia herself had inky blue-black hair, a deep purple tail, and icy blue eyes that glittered as she threw her head back and laughed.

"You're wasting your time, Effluvia. We don't even know where the pearl is," Layla said bravely.

"Pearl? Who said anything about a pearl?" Effluvia laughed again. "I'm here for the tropical talent show. I've been told

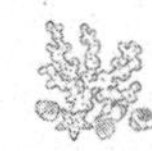

I have quite a lovely voice." She opened her mouth, and the girls reacted fast.

"Cover your ears!" Grace yelled. "Don't listen to her sing, or she'll put you under her spell!"

Sirens had very powerful songs that could make you do whatever they wanted. The Sea Keepers had almost been hypnotized by Effluvia's song before, but luckily

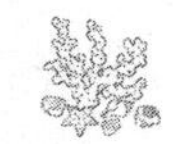

Marina and some dolphins had managed to save them just in time. But many other creatures hadn't been so lucky.

"How rude," Effluvia sneered.

"The talent show is only open to sea creatures anyway," Tarni called.

"Hmm, in that case, my new friend would like to compete," Effluvia said. "Come here, my little fishy!" she sang.

Grace frowned. Effluvia was definitely up to something!

Sure enough, from across the reef they heard the sound of screaming—and then an enormous shark swam into the theater! It was huge, with a pointed nose and rows of sharp teeth that made Grace shudder in fright. Its back and fins were covered with a pattern of dark-gray stripes. It was even

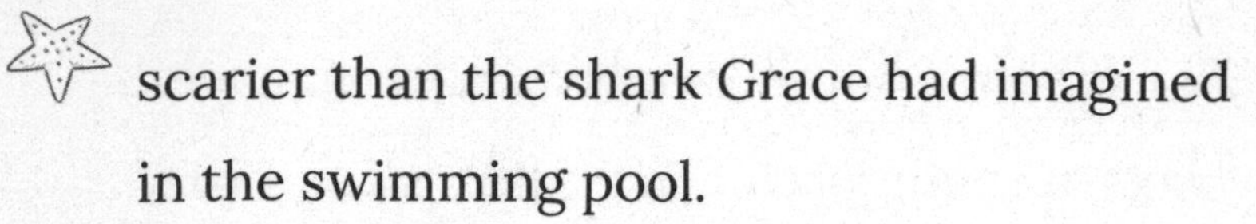

scarier than the shark Grace had imagined in the swimming pool.

As the shark swam closer, she couldn't help looking into its terrifying eyes, and there she saw something even scarier—a strange gleam. The shark was under Effluvia's control!

"Arrgggh!" the octopus screamed, dropping juggling shells everywhere as the shark swam past. The flamenco-dancing crabs ran off sideways, and the crustacean band abandoned their instruments and scuttled into the reef as fast as they could. The busy theater was suddenly silent as all the fish hid among the coral.

"Don't worry, that's a tiger shark, and they don't eat mermaids," Marina whispered to the girls.

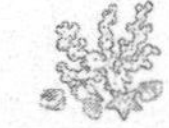

"I'm sure I could get him to make an exception for you," Effluvia said with a nasty grin. "But first, I have a job for him. Shark! Destroy the theater!"

"No!" Tarni gasped.

The shark bit the coral arch with its sharp teeth. The coral cracked and crumbled. Then the shark swam up to the seaweed garland and tore it down, grabbing it with its jaw and shaking its head from side to side, like a dog with a bone.

Grace couldn't watch any more. "Stop it!" she yelled, swimming as fast as she could toward the shark. Up close, it was even more scary. It was three times as long as she was, sleek and powerful, with huge, pointy teeth.

What am I doing? Grace thought as she

grabbed its smooth, slippery tail. She could hear her friends yelling her name as she tried to pull the shark away from the stage, but he wouldn't budge. "I said, STOP!"

The shark turned and looked at her, then flicked its tail. Grace couldn't hold on any longer. She shot through the water and landed with a bump on the special thrones the mermaids had made for Queen Adrianna and King Caspian.

Effluvia laughed and clapped her hands. "Ooh, yes, get those thrones too!" She sang a high note, and the shark turned toward Grace.

The shark lunged at her with its mouth open wide. Grace dove out of the way just as the shark bit down on one of the thrones. As it chomped and munched, Grace sped back to the others.

"Why are you doing this, Effluvia?" shouted Layla.

Effluvia shrugged. "It's fun! Besides, I know you goody two-fins won't be able to resist helping the poor *fishy wishies* so they

can have their silly show. And while you're busy doing that, I'll be finding the Golden Pearl. Come, Fang!" Effluvia laughed again and swam away, Fang trailing behind her.

Layla groaned dramatically. "The worst thing is, she's right! We *do* have to help save the show." They all looked over at where the striped shark was still tearing into the thrones with his sharp pointed teeth.

"We have to stop him!" said Grace.

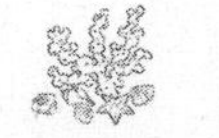

Chapter Five

As the shark ripped the sea anemones away from the thrones, Grace noticed something...a pair of googly eyes sticking out of the sand. "That's it," she whispered to herself.

"What's it?" Layla asked.

"What do you call an electric ray who's going to save the day?" Grace said to the others.

"Um, what?" Marina looked confused.

"Raymond!" Grace pointed to where the ray was still hidden in the sand. "He

can use his electric power to shock the shark! Come on!"

Marina and the girls swam over to where the ray was buried.

"Raymond, come out, we need your help," Layla told him.

"Are you joking? There's an enormous shark out there!" Raymond's muffled voice came out of the sand. "No, thank you very much. I don't fancy being a shark snack. I'm staying right here."

"But it's destroying the theater!" Grace said.

"Please, Raymond," Emily added.

"Can't you just give him a little shock?" pleaded Marina.

The sand shook as Marina spoke. "Is that…a royal command?" Raymond asked.

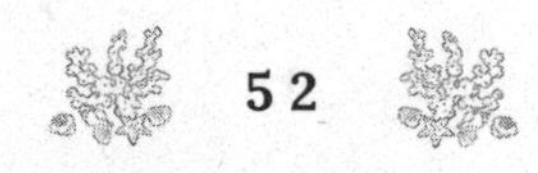

Marina glanced at the girls and winked. "Yes!" she said. "A very important royal command! The queen, king, and I would be very, very grateful if you could do this enormous favor for us..."

The sand trembled again, and Raymond rose up in the water and bowed. "It would be my honor, Princess." Then he looked at the shark, busy destroying the thrones. "Him?" he squeaked. "He's massive!"

"Wait!" Grace said. "He's big, but you're powerful."

"Please," Emily said gently, "you're the only one who can help."

"Atlantis is counting on you," Marina added.

"Oh, go on then," Raymond said reluctantly. "I'll try. For you, Princess."

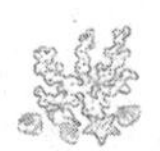

Nervously, the ray flapped his wings and swam toward the shark, who had finished attacking the thrones and was biting through more of the seaweed garland.

"Couldn't stay nice and safe," Raymond grumbled as he swam over. "Had to risk tail and fin to try and help the princess." His skin started to ripple and glow blue with electric power. "He's definitely going to eat me!"

"You can do it!" Layla said in a stage whisper.

Raymond glowed brighter and brighter, and the girls could hear the buzz of electricity around him. Then he reached out a fin and touched the shark's tail. Blue light coursed over the tiger shark's striped skin.

"AARRGGHHH!" The shark jumped. "WHO DID THAT?"

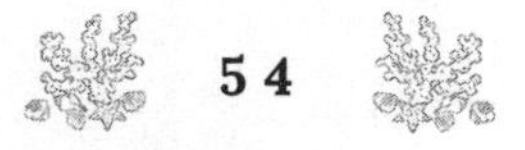

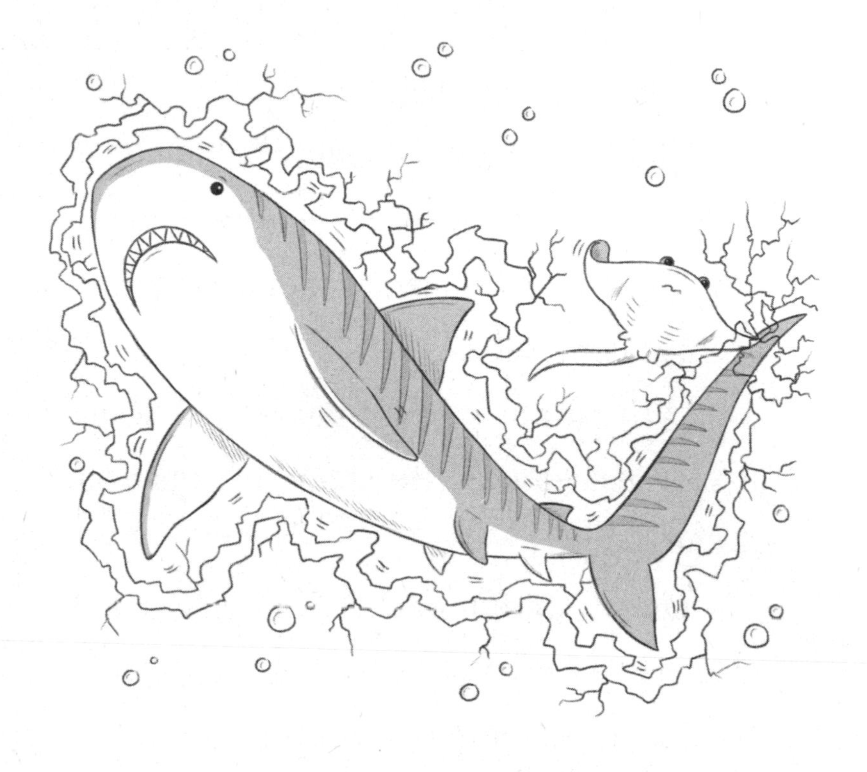

Raymond scurried down to the sand and buried himself.

Grace sped over. "It was us!" she declared. Marina, Layla, and Emily came and joined her.

"And we'll do it again if you don't leave," Layla added.

"Yeah!" cried Emily.

The Sea Keepers couldn't help feeling nervous as they faced the enormous tiger shark. But as he looked at them, the shark seemed confused.

"Where am I?" he asked. "And what have I just eaten?" He shook his head in disgust. "*Bleugh!*"

Grace stared into the shark's black eyes. They were still scary, but the hypnotized light had gone out of them. "I think the electric shock broke Effluvia's spell!" she said, grinning.

"What spell? *What is going on?*" the shark bellowed.

"It *was* her!" Layla pointed. They could see Effluvia and Fang searching the reef at the side of the theater's sandy clearing.

"She put you under a spell and made you attack the theater."

The shark looked around at the debris. Then he grabbed his tummy with his fins. "Ugh! I feel like I've eaten a load of rocks."

"Um, you did," Grace said, looking around at the wrecked theater. With a flick of his tail, the shark swam off. The mermaids sighed with relief.

"Raymond, you were great!" said Emily.

"Yes, thank you, my parents will be so grateful," Marina said, grinning.

"Hmmmm," Raymond said grumpily, burying himself even deeper in the sand in front of the stage. "Kindly go away now."

Tarni and Iluka swam over. "You did it!" cried Tarni, rushing over to hug them.

"But the theater is ruined," Layla said.

Iluka smiled. "That siren won't beat us," he said. "The tropical talent show will go ahead, even if the acts have to perform on a bare bit of seabed!"

But Effluvia was swimming toward them. There was a glint in her eye.

"Uh-oh," whispered Grace. "I don't think she's finished making trouble."

"Stupid shark," said Effluvia, scowling

at them. "But we all know there's only one creature who can *really* destroy the oceans...humans! Since the talent show means so much to you, why don't we make sure that *they* can see it too?"

Laughing wickedly, she swam down to the nearest bit of coral and snapped it off. The mermaids winced. Then Effluvia swam up to the water's surface, where the shimmering rainbow bubble protected the theater from human eyes.

"What's she going to do?" Layla gasped.

With a cruel smile, Effluvia used the spiky coral to burst the magical bubble. POP! For a second the theater shimmered with light, and then the bubble was gone.

"Oh, look," Effluvia said, pointing up at the surface. "There's a shadow—I think

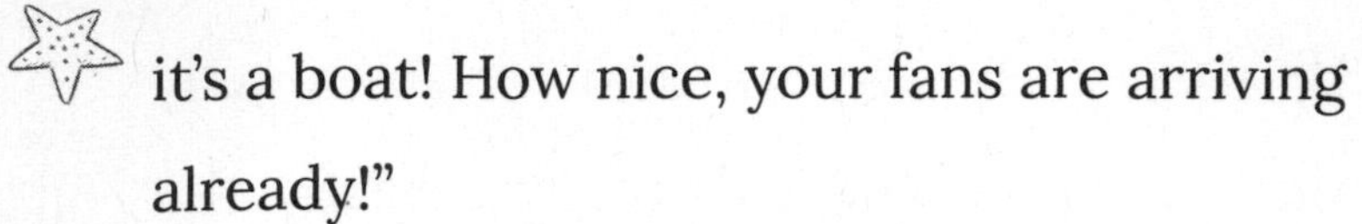

it's a boat! How nice, your fans are arriving already!"

"Humans!" Marina and Tarni shot to the surface. Grace followed as fast as she could, with Emily and Layla just behind her. Carefully poking their heads above water, they spotted a boat coming closer.

"It doesn't look like a fishing boat," Grace said as she peered at it.

"There's some writing on the side, but I can't quite see..." Emily said.

"*Barrier Reef Scuba Tours*," Grace read out grimly. "Oh no, they're divers!"

Sure enough, the people on the boat were putting on flippers, scuba masks, and oxygen tanks.

"What are we going to do?" Tarni cried. "The divers are going to see the theater!"

Chapter Six

Effluvia popped up at the surface. "What's wrong, got stage fright?" she sneered. "Well, I'm off to find the pearl. Enjoy the show—break a fin!" She swam back down to the reef, laughing.

The mermaids looked at each other in horror. "Can we make a new bubble to protect the theater?" Emily asked.

Tarni shook her head. "It's very powerful magic. It took months to make the first one."

“There’s only one way to save the show,” said Grace. “We have to find the Golden Pearl before Effluvia and use its magic to fix the theater and the bubble. We need to solve that riddle,” she declared.

Next to her, Emily, Layla, and Marina nodded.

They swam down to where Iluka was busy trying to repair the thrones. Now that the shark had gone, all the creatures that lived in the reef were coming back out. Tropical fish swam around the theater, helping the mermaids gather up the seaweed garland. The octopus was collecting his juggling shells, and the members of the crustacean band were sidling back toward their instruments.

“Iluka, did you have any ideas about

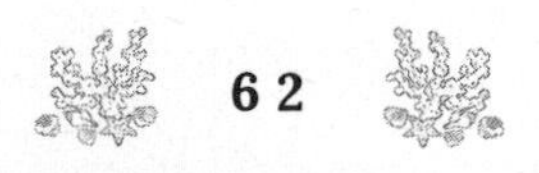

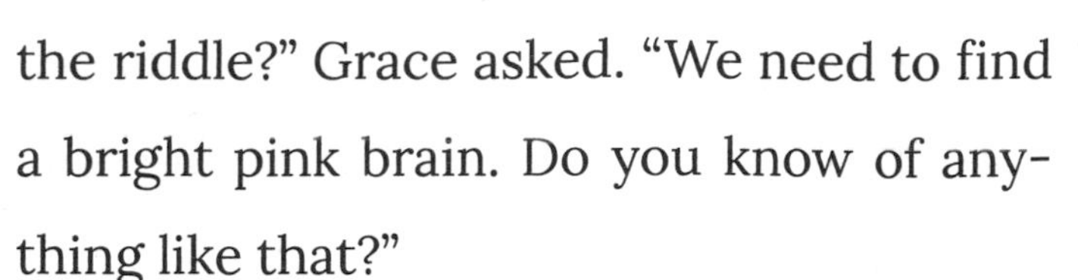

the riddle?" Grace asked. "We need to find a bright pink brain. Do you know of anything like that?"

Iluka stroked his beard thoughtfully. "It could be the brain coral. But that's not pink, it's white."

"The riddle says 'look for one of brightest pink.'" Layla shook her head. "If the brain coral is white, that can't be it. Is there anything else that's pink? Or brainy?"

"Some sea fan coral is pink," Tarni said.

"So are some anemones," Iluka added. "But I wouldn't call them brainy. Are we sure the old clam remembered it right?"

A thought was forming in Grace's mind. "That's it!" she cried. "The Mystic Clam is old—really, really old. Didn't you say the coral is getting bleached white? Maybe

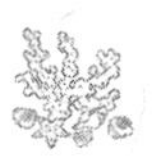

hundreds and hundreds of years ago, back when the clam remembers the pearls being hidden, the brain coral was bright pink!"

"Great idea, Grace," Emily said.

"Brilliant brainpower," Layla joked.

"The brain coral is on the reef just outside the theater. I'll show you the way," Tarni offered. "Come on!"

"Hang on, where's Effluvia?" Grace said.

"Over there," Layla pointed across the reef to a purple tail sticking out of the coral as Effluvia searched for the pearl.

She was surrounded by a crowd of tiny orange clown fish, who were darting in and out of the anemones, directed by Fang.

"She must have enchanted them to help her look!" Emily cried.

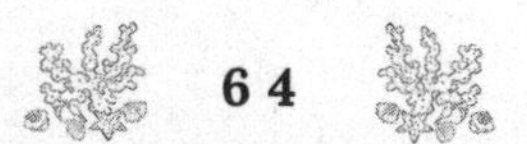

“Let’s pretend we’re still trying to fix the theater,” Grace whispered.

“We need to get some seaweed to make more garland,” Layla said loudly.

“Oh, yes. There is more seaweed just outside of the theater, Sea Keepers,” Tarni bellowed awkwardly. She winked at the girls as she pointed the way to the brain coral.

They swam across the theater, trying not to make it look like they were hurrying. Once they were outside, they rushed toward a busy reef, filled with anemones and fish.

"Tarni said it was just outside the theater..." Grace muttered.

"Hmm, let me guess, is it that thing that looks like a massive brain?" Layla said.

Grace couldn't help grinning. The brain coral was a massive ball, taller than Marina standing on the tips of her fins, and covered in squiggly ridges and wrinkles all over its white surface. It really did look like a big brain!

"I bet it looked even more amazing when it was bright pink," Emily said. "I just hope this is the answer to the riddle."

“There’s only one way to find out...” Grace said. She started to swim around the huge coral, looking in all the grooves and wrinkles for a magical glow. Emily, Layla, and Marina searched too.

“Queen Nerissa chose some good hiding places!” Marina muttered.

“Let’s be organized,” Grace told her friends. “Take a section each and search it slowly from the base to the top.”

Grace swam to the bottom of the coral, down by the seabed. None of them spoke as they peered carefully into the folds of the coral, looking for a flash of gold.

As she worked her way slowly up to the top of the coral, Grace started feeling frustrated. Where *was* it? Maybe they’d

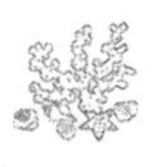

gotten the riddle wrong and the pearl was hidden somewhere else entirely…

But just as she was beginning to worry, her eye caught sight of something glowing, deep inside a ridge. She tried to put her hand in, but it was too big, and she didn't want to hurt the delicate coral.

"I think I see it!" she whispered to the others.

"Um, that's not the only thing... I can see some divers!" Emily gulped, pointing behind Grace.

Grace turned around. Up at the surface, she could still see the shadow of the boat. As they watched, a diver plopped into the water next to it. Then two others jumped in and they clustered around the boat, their flippers making waves while they arranged their fancy-looking camera equipment.

"We have to hide," Marina whispered, her face pale.

"But the pearl—" Grace looked down at where the pearl was embedded in the coral. They nearly had it! She tried again to squeeze her hand into the ridge, but it was no good. She couldn't reach the pearl.

Marina shook her head. "We'll come back for it later."

But we're so close! Grace thought. She didn't want to leave the pearl, but Marina looked so worried that she nodded.

Before Marina could usher them away, there was a familiar laugh.

"So, the pearl is in this coral." Effluvia laughed. "You might have found a big brain, but you aren't very clever—you've led me right to it!"

"Effluvia, you'd better hide. There are divers," Marina said, trying to reason with her. "Even sirens don't want to be seen by humans."

"You brought these *two-legs* into our kingdom!" Effluvia spat.

"They're different!" Marina protested.

"The divers have cameras—they'd tell the whole world about us."

Effluvia waved a hand. "You'd better go and hide then. I'm going to get the pearl!" She threw her head back and laughed. "And I don't have to go near those stupid divers to do it... Clown fish, search the coral!"

"Yeah, you heard her—go get it!" Fang commanded them.

The tiny clown fish surrounded the brain coral. They were so small they could swim right into the tightest ridges and folds, where Grace's hand wouldn't fit.

Grace held her breath. It was only a matter of time before one of the clown fish found the pearl! Just then a shadow passed over her head, and she ducked behind some coral.

"Diver!" she hissed. But it wasn't a diver—it was the tiger shark! He circled the coral and swam back to Effluvia, gnashing his teeth. The clown fish sped out of the coral like a cloud of butterflies and hid behind the siren.

"You made me eat the theater," the shark snapped at Effluvia. "You hypnotized me."

Effluvia gave a nervous laugh. "My fishy friend! I was—"

"I'm not your friend." The shark interrupted her. "But I *am* hungry..." He circled around Effluvia, and the siren actually looked worried.

"Now listen—" Effluvia opened her mouth to sing, but the shark bared his teeth and she let out a squeal instead. "Get away from me, you toothy idiot. Argh!"

As the shark snapped at her, Effluvia swam off as fast as she could, Fang and the clown fish trailing behind her.

"And don't come back! I'll be waiting!" the shark yelled.

"Yes!" Layla cheered. But the shark was turning to them with his mouth open wide and a hungry look in his eye...

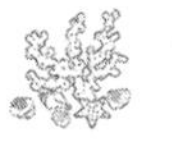

"Stop! Don't eat us!" Grace yelled as the fierce tiger shark swam toward them.

Chapter Seven

The girls quickly ducked behind the brain coral as the huge shark swam toward them. But as he began to circle the coral, there was nowhere to hide!

Oh no, thought Grace. *We're going to be a shark snack.*

But to their surprise, the shark said, "Don't worry, I'm not going to eat you. I still feel sick from eating that theater! *Bleurgh!*" He swam around and around the brain coral.

"I think I remember reading that sharks have to keep moving all the time," Emily whispered. "They can't stop, or they'll drown."

As she watched the shark swimming, Grace had an idea. "Would you mind scaring off the divers?" she asked him. "We need to get the pearl without them seeing us."

"But please don't eat them!" Emily exclaimed.

"I don't eat divers," the shark scoffed. "My dad ate one of their bubble shells once and it gave him hiccups for a week."

"I think he means oxygen tanks," Layla giggled.

"Uggggh, that theater was rock hard," the shark moaned and spat something

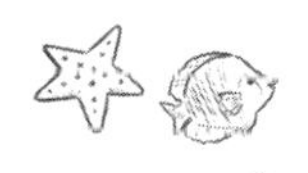

out—a tooth! It sank down through the water, and Grace dove to catch it.

"Are you okay?" Emily asked.

The shark flicked his tail happily. "Don't worry, it'll grow back. Do you think the humans will put me on TV? My cousin was a movie star, you know? *Duh-duh, duh-duh.* Here I come..."

The girls peeked over the coral as the tiger shark approached the divers, humming to himself as he went.

The first diver saw him and let off a cloud of bubbles as he frantically made signals at the others. They splashed to the surface as fast as they could, then disappeared into the boat. The tiger shark circled a few times, splashing and gnashing his teeth. Then he

turned back to the girls and gave them a toothy grin.

"They won't be back in the water any time soon," Marina laughed.

They quickly swam to where Grace had seen the pearl's golden light. It was still there!

"But how are we going to get it out?" Layla asked. She stuck her hand in, but like Grace's, it was too big. Luckily, Grace was still holding something smooth and pointy—the shark's tooth.

"Maybe this will help!" she said. She put the sharp edge into the coral. It was just long enough to reach the pearl! She used the tooth to gently work the pearl out of its hiding place.

"Almost...there...yes!" she cried as the pearl fell into her palm.

Grace cupped the glittering golden pearl in her hands. Emily and Layla reached out to touch it, and the three friends grinned at each other.

"I wish for the theater and the magic bubble to be fixed!" Grace said happily.

As the golden light vanished from the pearl, a rainbow of magic shot through the water and arched over the theater, protecting it in a shimmering bubble once again.

"You did it!" cheered Marina.

"Let's go back to the theater," Layla said.

"Thank you!" Emily called to the shark as they left.

"You're welcome," the tiger shark yelled back. "Just let me know if I become famous!"

They swam over to the sandy clearing. The theater looked just as wonderful as it had before, with a colorful coral arch over the stage and bright anemones covering the thrones. Tarni and Iluka raced up to greet them.

"Good work, Sea Keepers! I couldn't have done it better myself," Iluka cheered.

"And just in time!" Tarni nodded to a wave of bubbles heading toward them.

"Now *that*'s the royal carriage!" Marina said, grinning as the bubbles parted to reveal an incredible conch shell carriage, pulled by two dolphins. Inside it, waving regally, were King Caspian and Queen Adrianna.

"Mom! Dad! Kai!" Marina yelled, swimming over to stroke her dolphin friend. Kai clicked excitedly, delighted to see her.

Grace, Emily, and Layla bowed low as the royals swam down from the carriage. Queen Adrianna had blue hair and a red tail, and King Caspian had a blue tail and green hair and beard. They were both wearing incredible crowns made of plaited seaweed and pearls.

"Marina! Sea Keepers!" Queen

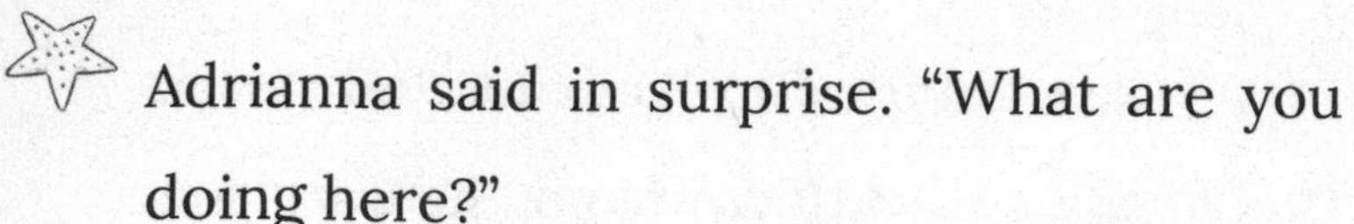

Adrianna said in surprise. "What are you doing here?"

"We found another Golden Pearl, Your Majesty," Layla announced.

"And we stopped Effluvia!" Emily chimed in.

"We fixed the theater too, so it's ready for the tropical talent show!" Grace added, feeling proud.

"It sounds like you've been very busy," said King Caspian.

"Welcome, Your Majesties." Iluka gave a deep bow. "Let me show you to your seats."

"I'm going to stay with Kai. We've got lots to catch up on," Marina said, hugging her dolphin friend.

As the royals swam off, Tarni turned to the girls, grinning with excitement.

"Sea Keepers, would you do us the honor of judging the tropical talent show? After all, it wouldn't even be happening without you."

"We'd love to!" Layla said excitedly.

Tarni gave them seats right next to the royal thrones. The theater was filling up with tropical mermaids, along with fish, sea turtles, and other sea creatures from the reef. Everyone was thrilled that the theater was fixed, and excited for the show to begin. But there was someone missing...

"Hang on!" Grace had a sudden thought. "Raymond!"

"Excuse us, sorry, sorry," Layla said as they swam through the audience, toward the front of the stage.

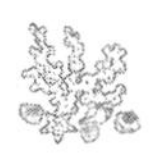

"Raymond, are you still here?" Emily called.

There was a flurry of sand and Raymond appeared.

"The show's about to start, and you have to be in it," Grace said firmly. "If you're brave enough to zap a tiger shark, then you're brave enough to tell your jokes in front of an audience."

"Yeah!" Layla agreed.

Raymond looked as if he was thinking. Suddenly he clapped his wings together. "I'll do it!" he said. "I'll go get ready."

The girls grinned at him then rushed back to their seats just as Tarni came onstage.

"Welcome, everyone, to the two hundredth tropical talent show!" Tarni announced. The crowd clapped and cheered and

drummed their tails against the sandy floor. The girls joined in, beaming with delight.

"I now present our first act, the Seahorse Superstars!" Tarni swam to the side, clapping, as a troop of seahorses swam onstage.

Grace, Layla, and Emily watched in wonder as the seahorses swam across the

stage like synchronized swimmers, dancing through the water in perfect unison.

"Oooh! Ahhhh!" The crowd cheered as the seahorses linked tails to form the shape of a star, then arranged themselves to look like a jellyfish with waving tentacles.

The next acts were great as well.

The juggling octopus didn't drop any of his shells, and the flamenco crabs performed so well that Grace jumped up and gave them a *swimming* ovation. Then there was a starfish who cartwheeled and flipped like a gymnast. Grace's hands hurt from clapping so much.

Finally, it was Raymond's turn. Grace crossed her fingers, hoping he would enjoy his moment in the spotlight.

Raymond swam onstage and blinked

at the crowd. For a second Grace thought he was going to bury himself in the sand again. But then he coughed and started his act. "Hello, everyone! It's great to *sea* you all here today..."

Every joke he told made the crowd laugh until they all had tears rolling down their faces. Even King Caspian and Queen Adrianna were holding their bellies as they roared with laughter.

When Raymond finally finished and bowed, the merfolk clapped and cheered so loudly that the whole theater shook. Raymond's performance had been... electrifying!

Tarni returned to the stage. "We have some very special guests to judge the talent show tonight," she said. "Our Sea Keepers—Layla, Grace, and Emily! Please make your decision, Sea Keepers, and then join us onstage to announce the winner!"

Grace, Emily, and Layla gathered together.

"The seahorses were amazing," Layla said.

"And the juggling octopus was really impressive too," Emily added.

"But there was one act everyone loved the most," Grace said. The others nodded.

"Let's go!" Layla said. She swam onstage, waving to everyone as she went.

Emily looked as if she wanted to bury herself in the sand like Raymond. Grace grabbed her hand and Emily smiled gratefully. Emily hated being the center of attention as much as Layla loved it!

"All the acts were so, so good," Layla declared.

"It was a very hard decision," Emily added shyly.

"But there was one that stood out," Grace continued. "Not only is he the funniest fish we've ever met, but his bravery also stopped the shark attack. The winner of this year's tropical talent show is...Raymond!"

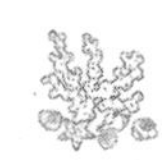

Chapter Eight

Queen Adrianna and King Caspian swam onstage, followed by Marina and Kai. With a dazzling smile, the queen presented Raymond with a gleaming rainbow-colored shell trophy.

"Your majesties." Raymond did a wobbly bow. "I am your humble servant."

"What a wonderful show!" King Caspian boomed. "And excellent work finding another Golden Pearl, Sea Keepers." The royals turned to them and, to Grace's

relief, Queen Adrianna didn't look fierce at all.

"Yes," Queen Adrianna said. "I must say, you are doing very well as Sea Keepers. Perhaps the magic *did* know what it was doing when it chose you."

The girls grinned at the compliment. "But there are still more Golden Pearls out there," Adrianna said firmly. "And Effluvia won't rest until she finds one."

"We won't let her," Grace promised.

"As soon as the Mystic Clam remembers where another pearl is hidden, we'll come back," Emily said.

"Maybe for the talent show next year as well!" Layla added.

Adrianna nodded her head. "I know we can rely on you, Sea Keepers." Then she

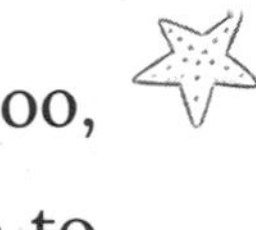

turned to Marina. "Well done to you too, my daughter. I wonder, would you like to join us for the next stage of our royal tour?"

"Oh, yes, please!" Marina squealed, giving Kai a big hug.

"Say your goodbyes and meet us by the carriage," King Caspian said, his eyes twinkling. "Farewell, Sea Keepers. Keep up the good work."

Marina did a happy dance as soon as her parents' backs were turned.

"No more annoying Neptune bossing me around!" she whooped. "But I'll go back to Atlantis soon and check on the Mystic Clam. And you should go home too."

Grace, Emily, and Layla looked at each other. It was always strange going home after an amazing mermaid adventure!

They hugged everyone goodbye and waved to Raymond, and then Marina sang the song to take them home:

"Send the Sea Keepers back to land,
Until we need them to lend a hand."

A whirlpool of bubbles surrounded them as the magic whisked them away from the coral reef and back into the changing rooms at the swimming pool.

As the smell of chlorine hit Grace, she realized she was still in her swimsuit with her towel wrapped around her. No time had passed while they'd been gone. It was only minutes ago that she'd won her race—even though they'd just had a whole mermaid adventure!

"That was incredible!" Emily said.

"Remember the look on Effluvia's face when the shark chased her away?" Layla said with a giggle.

The girls laughed and joked together as Grace got changed. But when they came back out onto the side of the pool and

spotted Grace's brother, Henry, with the sub-aqua club, their smiles faded.

The club's members were all in their flippers and snorkels, and some of the older ones were wearing full wet suits and oxygen tanks, just like the divers they'd seen exploring the Great Barrier Reef. Grace knew that her friends were thinking the same thing she was.

"We need to talk to the divers," she said. "They probably don't realize how much damage they could do to the coral if they dive near a reef. I'm sure they would be careful if they knew."

"Layla, you do it, you're the best at talking to people!" Emily said.

"Let's all do it together," Grace suggested. "We can be brave like Raymond!"

They walked over to the divers. "Excuse me, can we talk to the group about coral?" Grace asked the instructor. "It's really important."

"Of course!" The instructor sounded surprised, but she clapped her hands and yelled, "Gather around, everyone. These girls have something they want to tell us about."

"Coral is a living creature. It might look hard and strong, but it's really fragile. You shouldn't touch it at *all*," Layla told them. "No matter how tempting it might be."

"Always be careful with your flippers," Emily added, "so that you don't accidentally brush against it. A whole section of reef can die if just one small piece is damaged."

"Coral is really important to the

ecosystem," Grace told them. "So it's very important to protect it." The divers all nodded.

"And one last thing... If you see a mer-maid, make sure you keep it a secret!" Layla joked.

"Thank you, girls, that was extremely informative," the instructor said.

The diving group clapped and Grace, Layla, and Emily smiled at each other. They knew Tarni and the other mermaids would be proud of them, and they felt sure Henry and his friends would be careful if they ever snorkeled near a coral reef.

When Henry's lesson was over, they all went back to Grace's house. Her family lived in a pretty stone cottage, right next to the sea, with her granddad's boat moored nearby and lobster pots stacked outside.

It was cold and dark, and they could hear the wind howling outside, but the cottage felt like the coziest place in the world. Grace's dog, Barkley, curled up under the table as her mom brought out a vegetable lasagna from the oven, its top covered in bubbling golden cheese.

"Mmmmmmm!" the girls exclaimed. "Dive in, everyone. I've made a lot."

Grace's mom served her daughter a big portion. "I know swimming always makes you hungry."

Layla, Emily, and Grace exchanged a

grin. Grace's mom had no idea that they'd *all* been swimming today!

Mom poured them glasses of water and then raised hers in the air. "To Grace's win and Henry's first snorkeling lesson!" she toasted.

As happy chatter filled the kitchen, Layla leaned over to her friends. "Here's to finding another Golden Pearl!" she whispered to them.

"And defeating Effluvia!" added Emily.

"And to having another mermaid adventure soon!" finished Grace, clinking glasses with her fellow Sea Keepers.

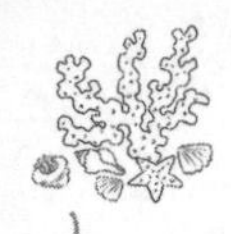

How to Be a Real-Life Sea Keeper

Would you like to be a Sea Keeper just like Emily, Grace, and Layla? Here are a few ideas for how you can help protect our oceans and the environment.

1. Reuse gift bags.

If you get a present in a gift bag, save the bag and use it again. That way it doesn't end up in the trash or in recycling.

2. Make a plastic bottle planter.

Instead of recycling a plastic bottle, cut it in half and decorate it however you'd like. Put some potting soil inside, and plant a flower or vegetable.

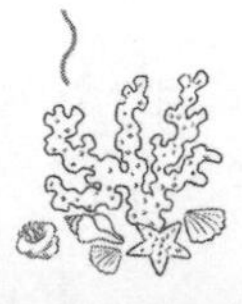

3. Ask your parents to buy green cleaning products.

Green cleaning products and laundry detergent clean your home naturally and are made using sustainable, non-toxic, ingredients.

4. Donate toys and games you no longer use.

Instead of throwing away old toys and games, donate them so they can be played with again.

5. Join your school's environmental or green club.

If there's not one, start your own! Ask your friends and teachers about what you can do to make your school more environmentally friendly.

Collect all the Sea Keepers books!

About the Author

Coral Ripley is the pen name of an author who works in children's publishing and has written a number of successful animal books. She cares passionately about the environment and the future of all creatures, big and small. Coral lives in London with her husband, baby daughter, and two cats.